Boise State University Western Writers Series   Number 44

Dorothy Johnson

By Judy Alter

Editors: Wayne Chatterton
James H. Maguire

Business Manager:
James Hadden

Cover Design and Illustration
by Arny Skov, Copyright 1980

Boise State University, Boise, Idaho

Copyright 1980
by the
Boise State University Western Writers Series

ALL RIGHTS RESERVED

Library of Congress Card No. 80-70458

International Standard Book No. 0-88430-068-4

Printed in the United States of America by
J & D Printing
Meridian, Idaho

Dorothy Johnson

Dorothy Johnson

I—Dorothy Johnson's Life and Career

Although her work is primarily rooted in her home state of Montana, Dorothy Johnson was not born a Westerner. Her birthplace was a farm in McGregor, Iowa, a town in the heart of the Midwest. Born on December 19, 1905, she was christened Dorothy Marie Johnson and called Marie by friends and family until she went to college.

But Marie Johnson did not stay in the Midwest long enough to absorb its culture or traditions. In 1908, a kidney ailment forced her father to give up farming. A year later, his search for office work and better health took the family west to Great Falls, Montana, and then to the temporary community of Rainbow Falls, where a dam and power plant were being built. The family lived in a tarpaper-covered freight depot. Drinking water had to be hauled from Great Falls, seven miles away.

Marie, at six, had just started school when the family moved to Rainbow Falls, where there was no school. "At six, you're still close to the ground. You can be fascinated by white pebbles the rain has washed and by the tumbling growth of prickly pear . . . . Trains went by our front window. Once there was a freight wreck that couldn't have been closer" ("Writer Recalls Childhood at Rainbow Dam," p. 4).

Formerly a teacher, Marie's mother taught her to read and write, and it was in Rainbow Falls that the future author wrote her first story. "I only got a couple of sentences down and it was just too hard to spell. I didn't write any more for a few years" ("The Years and the Wind and the Rain: A Biography of Dorothy Johnson," p. 14).

In 1912, the family moved from the prairie country of Rainbow Falls to Whitefish, a railroad town located forty miles south of the Canadian border in heavily timbered mountains. When Marie was entered in the Whitefish schools, her home tutoring proved so successful that she was ahead of her class and eventually wound up going through school two years younger than her classmates.

Although classmates later remembered her as studious and always reading, one also recalled a tomboy who was ready to play ball, ride a horse, or shoot marbles. At the age of ten, she read and disliked *Ben Hur*, and then she read *Tess of the Storm Country* because she'd been told not to. Johnson attributed her voracious reading habits to a doctor who predicted that her severe eye problems might cause blindness by the time she reached the age of twenty. She felt she had to read everything while she still could ("The Years," pp. 23-24).

Lester Johnson died in 1915, just before his daughter's tenth birthday. Left to support themselves, Marie and her mother realized that a college education for her was essential. Mrs. Johnson worked at two jobs, and Marie worked at anything she could. She ran errands, washed dishes, and even raised vegetables. At the age of fourteen, she became a relief operator at the telephone office. "To this day," she wrote, "when the timer on my electric range buzzes, I jump a foot" ("Number Please: Confessions of a Teen-Aged Central," p. 54).

In high school, Marie Johnson began to take her writing more seriously. One of her poems was published in the school yearbook, and with a friend she wrote a farce called "The Lively Life of Leon," with a popular classmate as the hero. She also took over her mother's job as a stringer for *The Kalispell Inter Lake,* but she later described herself as having been a poor reporter because she was too scared to ask questions of strangers. The experience, however, proved the basis for "First Date," a story published in *Collier's* in 1949 ("The Years," p. 42).

In the fall of 1922, she enrolled at Montana State University in Bozeman as a pre-med major, and on college registration forms her name appeared as Dorothy. Later, she confessed to a romantic notion about women physicians that led her into medicine although she was not the type to follow that career ("The Years," p. 47). Her poor grades in qualitative analysis and her dread of dissecting a cat helped her decide to transfer to the University of Montana in Missoula where she majored in English and turned her attention toward writing.

In Missoula, Professor Harold G. Merriam had begun a campus literary magazine, *The Frontier*. Submitted materials were subjected to a stern critique before acceptance, and Dorothy Johnson was elated to have four poems accepted in 1924. The first, "Marjory," was published in the winter issue; the other three were submitted in mid-winter, just before a nervous breakdown forced her to leave school. That breakdown, attributed to social pressures, financial worries, and a bad cold that she could not shake, kept her out of school for a year and a half.

She did not stop writing poetry during her time out of school, and three more pieces were accepted by *The Frontier*. Saying that her poetry was more in the nature of statements, Professor Merriam described her early work as "not symbolic, not highly imaginative, but a response to things she had seen, like a lost mine or a ghost town. It was a little nostalgic" ("The Years," p. 51). Toward the end of 1926, after she had returned to the university, her interest inexplicably turned to prose. "I suddenly became *not* a poet. I began to think differently. I began to think in terms of short stories. It all had to do with emotion or the expression of emotion. Somehow, the channeling of my emotion changed to short stories" ("The Years," p. 59).

Her biographer, Stephen Smith, suggests that Merriam influenced her in the direction of prose because, as he later commented, he could see at the time that her real talent lay in stories rather than verse ("The Years," pp. 58-59). Merriam, himself strongly interested in regional literature, may also have influenced her later choice of subject matter, a speculation strengthened by the dedication to him of *Indian Country,* a collection of her short stories. Published in *The Frontier* in 1927, Johnson's first short stories were "He'll Make A Good Sheriff" and "Happy Valley."

In her senior year, Dorothy Johnson received her first payment for a freelance submission. *Weird Tales* accepted a poem and paid twenty-five cents a line. She used up the pay buying issues of the magazine, at twenty-five cents a copy, watching for the poem to be published. Her senior year also marked a brief marriage to George William Peterkin, a soldier she had met on a blind date. The couple separated at her graduation and were later divorced.

Johnson missed her own commencement exercises because she was looking for a job in Spokane, Washington. She found one as a stenographer in a store in Okanogan, Washington. There, although she missed the creative atmosphere of the university, she kept working at her writing. She tried confession stories and hated them, and she couldn't bring herself to write Sunday School stories although the only other writer in Okanogan was earning $100 a piece for them ("The Years," p. 72). *The Frontier* published two more stories in 1930.

Dorothy Johnson liked Okanogan, but after more than two years, she felt the need to move on and went to Wisconsin where her mother and new stepfather lived. Within a few days of arriving in Waukau, she wrote a short story that had been brewing in her mind for several days. Called "Bonnie George Campbell," it brings together the lines from an English ballad and her impressions of a rodeo she had attended on an Indian reservation near Okanogan. Submitting her story to a Curtis Publishing Company magazine, *Country Gentleman*, she was surprised to have a reply from *The Saturday Evening Post*, another Curtis property. They paid $400—a fortune to an unemployed secretary—for her story and it was published in the issue of October 18, 1930.

In this short story, a cowboy named George Campbell proposes to his girl, Opal, but she wants more romance and less rodeo in her life. At a rodeo-picnic, an Eastern observer named Miss Burns helps Opal see George and rodeos in a different light, and the possibility that George might be injured convinces Opal that she wants to accept his proposal. The story's dialogue and background are authentic, especially when Opal explains such things as the cowboy wife's code of behavior to the outsider, but "Bonnie George Campbell" does not flow as smoothly as Johnson's later stories, and the device of a tenderfoot to whom things must be explained is one that she did not later need. She has called this formula piece a "come to realize" story (Letter from Dorothy Johnson, March 1980).

Several elements in this story anticipate the stories of her first published book, *Beulah Bunny Tells All*. Miss Burns, a photographer, serves in a capacity similar to Beulah Bunny's in that she, too, is an outsider who is able to see the action in a different perspective from that of the principal characters. Both women function in their stories as interpretive devices, but Miss Burns lacks the original and interesting character of Beulah. The ballad theme also appears frequently in the Beulah Bunny stories. It is used in Johnson's first story as a device to puzzle the naive heroine. Hearing Miss Burns quote the ballad "Bonnie George Campbell," Opal thinks the Easterner has made up a song about *her* George Campbell and is further moved to decide in the cowboy's favor.

The publication of "Bonnie George Campbell" seemed to assure her future, or so Johnson thought at the age of twenty-four. She had no way of knowing that it would be eleven years before she sold another story. Recently, she commented on one cause of that long dry spell, explaining that the editor who accepted "Bonnie George Campbell" wrote a wonderful letter of acceptance saying he was impressed with the unusual background of the story. "Like any beginner clutching at any straw, I took this to mean that stories with an unusual background had a better chance. So I wasted a lot of effort until 11 years later, when my mind went back to the same little corner of northern Washington that generated that story, and the series of 'modern Westerns' about Beulah Bunny resulted" (Letter from Dorothy Johnson, March 1980).

Johnson spent the next five years of the Depression working as secretary to the advertising manager of a paper-converting company in Menasha, Wisconsin. Writing direct mail copy about waxed paper and butter cartons was still writing, she reasoned (Letter from Dorothy Johnson, July 1980). Then, in 1935, she landed a job with the Gregg Publishing Company in New York. For the next nine years, she worked on the staff of Gregg's publication, *Business Education World*.

Dorothy Johnson loved New York, the pace, the museums, plays, and ferry rides. But she found making personal contacts difficult, and much of her off-hours time she devoted to her writing. In 1939, she set out to write a novel to prove that she could apply herself to writing at length. Writing 1,000 words a day, she turned out a 90,000 word manuscript that has never been published. "I found out I could do it," she told an interviewer ("The Years," p. 99).

By 1940, her fiction career seemed to have fizzled. But once again, Waukau proved to be a magic spot for her writing. She returned there for a vacation and spent her time working on a story idea that had come to her in New York. "Fellow Has to Get Away Some Time" proved to be the first of the Beulah Bunny stories in which Miss Bunny, a schoolteacher, is the narrator. Soon after she returned to New York, Johnson had three more Beulah Bunny stories written: "This Will Be Mine," "Going to Whittingham Fair," and "Cruel Barbara Ellen." She submitted them to *The Saturday Evening Post,* which bought all four for a then-unbelievable price of $2,100. This time, Dorothy Johnson's career was indeed launched. She wrote several more Beulah Bunny stories, all published in *The Post,* and in 1942 a collection of these stories became her first book, *Beulah Bunny Tells All,* published by the William Morrow Company.

By 1944, she was serving as advertising manager at Gregg, a job with a secure future but one which left her increasingly restless. She resigned to accept a position as managing editor of *The Woman,* a digest magazine which used reprints for about half its material.

Her production of short stories was high during the 1940s, and by the end of that decade her work was being published in a wide variety of magazines — *The Post, Seventeen, Argosy, Collier's, Cosmopolitan.* The stories written between 1941 and 1947 were mostly contemporary and several are set in war-time New York, but later ones, notably "The Man Who Shot Liberty Valance" (*Cosmopolitan,* June 1949), mark a change to Western subject matter. So did the second novel that she started in 1947: it would be ten years before that work saw publication as "The Hanging Tree." "To write about the West wasn't just some decision I sat down and made," she has said. "It was just what I happened to want to know about. Anytime I write anything that isn't the West of the 19th Century, I'm sort of off my track" ("The Years," p. 139).

Johnson also speculates that homesickness for the West had something to do with turning her attention to Western subjects. But though New York left her homesick, it also provided great opportunity for learning about the West. In the city's museums and libraries, she began to read and study about the Plains Indians. Her Western stories are not, she has emphasized, the result of listening to recollections of old timers in Whitefish. "The stories *they* told were about railroad wrecks and the Great Fire of 1910" (Letter from Dorothy Johnson, March 1979). Her stories are, instead, the result of a careful study of history.

With her new stories published in several magazines and her promotion to executive editor at *The Woman,* 1950 was a banner year for Johnson. But she was increasingly unhappy in New York. She loved its opportunities, but she never felt comfortable with its people. "New Yorkers just didn't act like the kind of human beings I was raised among in Montana" ("The Years," p. 142). And so she returned to Montana.

Johnson went to work for *The Whitefish Pilot* as a reporter and photographer. The drastic cut in pay she took to return to Montana made it necessary for her to sell her short stories regularly. Yet the early 1950s saw a decline in her sales, and she turned to articles in various non-fiction markets. Forty features for *Montana Parade* brought a scarce $10 apiece and were, she says, written "strictly from hunger" ("The Years," p. 179). The 1952 publication of "Journey to the Fort"—a story based on the memoirs of Fanny Kelly, a famous Indian captive—brought a resurgence of fiction sales, and earlier works began to appear in anthologies and foreign magazines.

In 1953, Johnson was offered the position of secretary/manager of the Montana Press Association in Missoula. She worked for the association for fourteen years and, for many of those years, also taught magazine courses at the University of Montana where she was an assistant professor of journalism. The big boon of 1953, however, was the decision of publisher Ian Ballantine to issue simultaneous hardcover and paperback collections of her Western short stories in a volume entitled *Indian Country.* Later printings of this book carry the title *A Man Called Horse*, after its final and most famous story. "The Hanging Tree," Johnson's first work to become a movie, was published in 1957. It had been ten years in the writing and re-writing and, when finished in the mid-50s, was a 65,000-word novel. Pared to a 39,000-word novelette, it was published, with nine other stories, by Ballantine in a collection called *The Hanging Tree*.

The year 1959 brought several honors to Johnson, including the celebration of Dorothy Johnson Day in Whitefish and her induction as an adopted member of the Blackfeet tribe. She was given the Indian name Kills Both Places. But 1959 also was a year in which Johnson recognized a change in the times: the short story market was dying, if not gone already, its demise brought about by the disappearance of the pulp magazines along with several weekly and monthly publications. According to Johnson, television killed these markets when people found it easier to watch than to read (Letter from Dorothy Johnson, July 1980). Her sales in the late 1950s were almost exclusively reprints, anthologies, and foreign publications. It was time for a career switch.

Johnson was not immediately attracted to the juvenile field, in spite of the recommendations of a friend who had published several books for young readers. The juvenile field, she felt, had a cloud over it. People apologized for writing juveniles as though it were clear they were incapable of doing anything else. But in the library, she found that some very respectable people were writing for young adults. "I decided it probably wasn't going to ruin any reputation I had acquired if I tried it" (Letter from Dorothy Johnson, March 1980). Her first juvenile, *Famous Lawmen of the Old West*, was published by Dodd, Mead and Company in 1963. Over the next sixteen years, she published a total of nine books for young readers.

In the early 1960s, Johnson's mother, who had been an invalid for seven years, died in a nursing home. Johnson was solely responsible for her hospital and medicine bills. But soon thereafter, the money from her second movie sale, "The Man Who Shot Liberty Valance," gave her a chance to travel during vacations. She went to the British Isles and Greece in 1961, Greece again in 1962, and Europe in 1963. Greece particularly fascinated her and became the subject of several of her young adult books.

In the late 1960s, the fast pace she had kept all her adult life was slowed by ill health, and in 1967 she resigned her position with the Montana Press Association. Her doctor faced her with the choice of giving up that position, teaching, or her own writing. "I couldn't quit writing; that was what I was working for" ("The Years," p 298). Retirement offered her the chance to do more of the traveling she loved, and her itinerary included the South Pacific, Australia, New Zealand, New Guinea, and Fiji. She went on a tour to Central America and on a European tour. Several weeks of travel through Africa ended with her fifth and last visit to Athens. A South American tour, marked by ill health, was her last trip outside this country.

Travel did not, however, keep her from writing, and the late 1960s and early 1970s saw publication of several of her works. After 1973, a four-year gap in publication covered a period during which her writing simply did not turn out to be published books. Several things went into her "lost cause file," including a murder-mystery set in Africa that was an outgrowth of her African tour several years earlier, and a young adult biography of Montana artist Charles M. Russell. Another disappointment for her was the failure to find a publisher for a series of articles about her childhood in Whitefish. She had reworked the articles, all previously published in *Montana*, into a collection and given them enough continuity, she felt, for publication as a book.

In 1977, Johnson published the first of two books that were to rival

"A Man Called Horse" and "The Hanging Tree" in importance in her career. *Buffalo Woman* is the biography of an ideal Sioux woman caught in the disintegration of the Sioux culture. Its sequel, *All the Buffalo Returning,* marks, to date, her last publication.

Although in poor health, Johnson is at work in 1980 on a new, non-Western title, *The Unbombed,* based on her experiences as an air raid warden in New York City during World War II.

Through the years, prestigious professional recognition has come to Johnson. The Alumni Association of the University of Montana gave her its Distinguished Service Award, and in 1973 the university awarded her an honorary Doctor of Letters. Western Writers of America voted her a Spur Award for the Best Western Short Story of 1956 for "Lost Sister," and in 1976 that organization presented her with its Golden Saddleman Award for her significant contribution to Western literature. In 1977, she received, for *Buffalo Woman,* the coveted Wrangler Award from the Cowboy Hall of Fame in Oklahoma City. In spite of these and other honors, Johnson still considers herself obscure (Letter from Dorothy Johnson, April 1980).

II — The Beulah Bunny Stories

Publication of *Beulah Bunny Tells All* marked a strong step forward in Johnson's career. "A writer," she wrote years later, "is not an author until he has produced a book. . . . Magazines are transitory. A book is permanent" ("When a Book Becomes a Movie," p. 11).

This volume consists of ten stories, most dealing with episodes involving Miss Bunny, a maiden-lady schoolteacher, and one or more of her former pupils. Six of the stories are about Strawberry Rowan, a young orphan cowboy who survives several years as a hobo and goes on to become a ranch owner and a famous but anonymous singer of ballads on the radio. Through the machinations of Miss Bunny, Strawberry is reunited with his high school sweetheart, Barbara Ellen, and they are happily married. Twice, figures from Strawberry's hobo past appear to endanger their happiness, and each time, Miss Bunny is in the thick of the action.

Other stories draw on Miss Bunny's own past. In "Blanket Squaw," she watches a parade and recognizes an older Indian woman whom she had known when both were young. Mary had moved freely in the white world and loved a white man but, as a sacrifice for his health, returned to the Indian life. Her grandson scoffingly tells Miss Bunny, "She wears a blanket. She doesn't even talk English" (p. 195). Another story, which tells of the cowboy who deserted Beulah for her own good when she wanted to run away with him, foreshadows a piece from *The Hanging Tree* collection, "The Last Boast," which uses the same theme. There are stories of Miss Bunny's matchmaking and even her arrest while masquerading as the fortune teller at a local carnival. The plots are often fantastic and the action, fast and sometimes nearly impossible.

Miss Bunny, a schoolteacher with a name so outrageous it twists the stereotype, narrates these stories, filling each with the force of her personality. Perpetually romantic and filled with a wry self-humor, Miss Bunny is a conniver and a manipulator of people, but she's funny and likeable enough to get away with it. A typical comment: "Generally I believe in letting the dead past bury its dead but if anybody wants to try resurrection, I'm willing to hold the lantern" (p. 87). Or, "I'm free to poke into other people's business whenever my conscience will allow — and my conscience in that respect is pretty elastic" (p. 4).

Although Johnson denies any autobiographical relationship to Miss Bunny (Personal letter, April 1979), many of Miss Bunny's experiences are clearly drawn from Johnson's own life. Specifically, her years in Okanogan are reflected in the sense of reality she imparts to Okanasket, and the use of ballads throughout the Strawberry Rowan stories reflects Johnson's strong personal interest in English ballads, earlier seen in the title to her first published story, "Bonnie George Campbell." Believing that the oral tradition brings the past closer and reflects the feelings of ordinary people seeking romance or adventure or entertainment, she has long been a student of ballads, which she plays on her ocarina, a small wind instrument ("The Years," p. 103). In the Beulah Bunny stories, Strawberry teaches Miss Bunny to play the ocarina, and then he sends her the songs he learns on the road. She later encourages him to collect them for publication. Other references to ballads abound in the stories. The names Strawberry Rowan (roan) and Barbara Ellen (Allen) are no accident, nor are such titles as "Going to Whittingham Fair" or "Cruel Barbara Ellen." Such extensive use of references to balladry seems, for Johnson, a way of finding continuity between ordinary people of the past and those of the present.

Amusing as they are, these stories lack the substance and dramatic appeal of the later short stories. The characters are ordinary people, meeting the challenges that daily life brings. In the later stories of *Indian Country* and *The Hanging Tree,* Johnson's characters are still ordinary people, but they meet and weather extraordinary challenges to their very survival. This book simply shows a lighter approach to life. But these are characters whose lives fascinated Johnson when she wrote about them. "I never meant to write a series," she later confessed, "but these were interesting people" (Letter from Johnson, March 1979). In the beginning of the Beulah Bunny volume, she denies her characters' reality: "All the characters in this book are purely imaginary. The author regrets this, because she would like to meet some of them."

Neither are the stories as strong in construction as her later work. The fantastic plots depend on acceptance of the character of Miss Bunny, and there is an overuse of coincidence in the fact that Miss Bunny is always present for the excitement, whether it's the attempted takeover of Strawberry's ranch by an old hobo or the wholesale arrest of carnival workers. In part, this coincidence can be explained by the fact that Miss Bunny, far from being a passive personality, actively seeks such situations. Also, these stories are set in contemporary times rather than in the past to which Johnson later turned. In spite of her firsthand knowledge of towns like Okanasket as they existed in the late 1920s, Johnson would later seem more at home writing about the last century, as she herself has said.

Still, the Beulah Bunny volume marks an important step not only in her prestige as an author but also in her development of her craft. Her ability to create a real, believable world and to present character and action in the confines of the short story was already clear.

III — The Collected Short Stories

Reviewers were quick to praise the originality of the *Indian Country* stories when the book was published in 1953. Writing for *The Saturday Review of Literature,* Seth Agnew said, "Here are Western stories at their best. There is no romanticizing of the noble savage, or of the intrepid pioneer. Here are credible men and women in credible situations. Here are stories told with pace and suspense and skill" (August 8, 1953, p. 16). And in *The English Journal,* John T. Frederick claimed, "Some of the best of this new Western fiction is contained in an unpretentious volume of short stories called *Indian Country* by Dorothy M. Johnson. These stories are marked by extraordinary economy of treatment and concentration of dramatic effect, by a quiet but consistent vitality in detail and diction" (September 1954, p. 282).

Four of the stories in *Indian Country* deal directly with the clash between Indian and white cultures, a theme that Elizabeth Ann James finds basic to many of Johnson's short stories ("A Thematic Analysis of Dorothy Johnson's Fiction," p. 39). "War Shirt" tells of a snobbish Easterner who comes West seeking the brother he long ago betrayed; he finds, instead, a proud Indian chief who denies any knowledge of him but who listens to his confession of past guilt and takes his gifts. The story dramatically illustrates the inability of the two cultures to understand each other. A variation of this theme is found in "The Unbeliever," in which an old white trapper returns to the Indian wife he left many years before. Never much of a success in the white world, Mahlon Mitchell is Iron Head to the Indians, a man with good medicine. Like many of her stories, this one is loosely based on fact. The source is the life of trapper James Beckwourth. In both stories, Johnson creates white men who deliberately chose to live as Indians for some part of their lives, and she makes this choice plausible. There was, she would have us know, much about the Indian culture that was good and strong.

Two stories, "Warrior's Exile" and "Scars of Honor," take place in the Indian world, and "Scars of Honor" is the only contemporary story in the collection. It involves young Indian men who, in the modern world, have lost the opportunity to sacrifice and prove their manhood in the old way. An ancient Indian helps lame Joe, rejected by the army, to earn his scars of honor in the way of the old religion. The story gives strong insight into the religion of the Cheyenne and includes a dramatic contrast between the Indian way of war and the white. "Warrior's Exile" also has to do with a dream vision that signified the growth to manhood for young Indian men. Having failed at two tries to dream, Smoke Rising has a strange and unusual experience on his third try, one that is regarded as mystical and that gives him the necessary medicine. This is one of a few stories by Johnson in which no element of white culture appears.

Four stories present life on the frontier from the white point of view. "Laugh in the Face of Danger," one of the slightest stories in the collection, consists of an old woman's reminiscences about her romance with an outlaw. "Beyond the Frontier" opens with the aftermath of an Indian raid, but the primary focus is on the growing romance between a cowboy and an Eastern girl, a different sort of a clash between cultures. Ever the romanticist, Johnson ends this one with a happy future forecast.

"Flame on the Frontier" is the story of a family attacked by Indians—father and older sons killed, mother and daughters captured, one young son escaped with the baby. Miraculously, the mother is freed and the two younger children safely returned. The story centers on the two daughters and their life as Indians. Mary Amanda, the oldest, dreams always of rescue and furtively talks to her younger sister in English to keep the language alive in the girl's mind. But when rescue comes, Mary Amanda stays with her Indian son and husband, because personal relationships are more important than cultural ties ("Thematic Analysis," p. 4). Sarah returns home. The ending of the story brings together the Indian whom Sarah had come to love and her white husband in a dramatic scene which makes it obvious that both men would do battle for her. The Indian offers her a place in his teepee, and her white husband threatens her with a frying pan. Johnson once explained the scene to an interviewer: "These were ignorant frontier people, the whites as well as the Indians . . . these people couldn't possibly have said, 'I love you'; it wasn't in them. But they understood what the situation was" ("Straight Talk in Missoula," p. 9).

Johnson credits this story to something she calls her "muse." Once she spent a day at the New York Public Library studying accounts of the New Ulm Massacre in Minnesota, and when she went to bed that night, her muse woke her up. "There was definitely a massacre going on where I was trying to sleep . . . these pictures and scenes kept crowding in" ("Straight Talk," pp. 8-9). Johnson gave up sleep and took notes in shorthand. Transcribing her notes the next day, she found they fell into scenes. Eventually, the short story resulted from these notes.

"Prairie Kid" is the powerful story of an eleven-year-old boy left as the man in charge to protect his sister and a young woman who cares for them. He proves his mettle by forcing an outlaw off the ranch at gunpoint. Another dramatic story in the collection is "Journey to the Fort," in which a captured white woman is being returned to the fort after ransom. Her thoughts are occupied with the fate of her daughter whom she helped escape from the Indians months earlier. Although Mrs. Foster's terror and her eventual relief are strongly felt, one student of Johnson's work has criticized this story for lacking sensitivity by portraying everything in black and white. According to James, the Indians here are purely evil, never shown with a human side as in other stories ("Thematic Analysis," p. 37). Johnson has pointed out, however, that anyone in Mrs. Foster's situation would indeed view Indians as purely evil. Her goal in this story was to recreate terror (Letter from Johnson, July 1980).

Two stories in this collection were made into movies, and both defy classification with the other stories. One is "The Man Who Shot Liberty Valance," the tale of the outcome of a clash between an Eastern tenderfoot and a bullying gunslinger, with its effect on the lives of the three central characters years later.

But the most remarkable story here is "A Man Called Horse," which Johnson wrote after reading Robert Lowie's *The Crow Indians*. The Crow way of life became so real to her that she felt that she could have lived in a Crow camp; then she got to wondering how someone from white culture would have survived among the Crow without having first read Lowie's book ("Straight Talk," p. 6). The story places a neurotic tenderfoot, totally ignorant of Indian ways, as a captive in an Indian camp and follows his growth to strong self-confidence as he builds for himself an honored place in the camp. Johnson is firm in her insistence that her hero did not find character in the wilderness. "You can only get acquainted with what's in yourself if you have something to begin with" ("Straight Talk," p. 7). Of a book with a similar plot in which a young man makes a grueling journey to find himself and returns unsatisfied, she wrote, "I cannot pity this empty man. He exasperates me . . . his world is blank. I cannot accept such heresy. Nobody's world is that bad" ("A Fruitless Search for the Meaning of Life," p. 11).

The stories of *The Hanging Tree* collection are similar in tone and setting to those in *Indian Country*, but there is less concentration on the clash between cultures, and when that theme appears, it is more subtle than brutal and dramatic as in "A Man Called Horse." One of the strongest of these stories is "Lost Sister," loosely based on the story of Cynthia Ann Parker, a Texas girl captured at the age of nine by Comanches and recaptured some twenty-five years later. Johnson once saw a picture of Cynthia Ann, taken shortly after her recapture, and thought hers the saddest face she'd ever seen ("Thematic Analysis," pp. 24-25). The events of "Lost Sister" grew out of her reaction to that picture, although the action in the story bears little relation to the real life of Cynthia Ann. Johnson's Indian/white woman eventually sacrifices herself for the sake of a grown son, an Indian chief, thereby showing the same strength that characterizes all of Johnson's major characters.

Two other stories deal loosely with Indian life and the clash between cultures. One is "Blanket Squaw," described earlier since it was also included in the Beulah Bunny collection. The other, "A Gift by the Wagon," tells of the reconciliation between a girl and her nephew whom she crippled years ago when stuffing him into a broken tree snag to hide from Indians. Young Basil finds he owes his life, not his lameness, to the girl, Fortune.

"The Last Boast," "The Man Who Knew the Buckskin Kid," and "I Woke Up Wicked" deal with outlaw life. The first is a short and somewhat macabre but strong story of a hanging scene, during which Wolfer Joe's final boast is of having once done one good thing by betraying a good woman and refusing to run away with her. The first sentence of this story clearly illustrates Johnson's use of prose rhythms to build tension and hold the reader: "When it came time for them to die, Pete Gossard cursed and Knife Hilton cried, but Wolfer Joe Kennedy yawned in the face of the hangman" (p. 22). "The Man Who Knew the Buckskin Kid" centers on an older rancher and his memories of an outlaw whose gang he almost joined at a low point in his life. Unlike other "obscure old men" (p. 42), John Rossum never boasted about having known the outlaw, and he is embarrassed by the questions of a young journalist. But the incident leads to a confession from his wife of many years which places on her the responsibility for having stopped Rossum from joining the outlaws. Like many of Johnson's characters, Mary Rossum had a gift for life to give without boasting, and John Rossum never knew all those years who let his horse out so that he couldn't ride with the gang. "I Woke Up Wicked" is one of Johnson's funnier stories, though she has admitted that the marvelous title was not her creation ("Straight Talk," p. 1). When he rode with the Rough String, Duke Jackson was an outlaw by mistake and always desperate to escape safely back to the honest life. But his final escape is managed and manipulated by one of the cleverest lady outlaws the West ever saw.

One story, using the theme of growth to maturity, echoes "The

Prairie Kid" of the earlier collection, though the boy's actions are never as openly heroic. In "A Time of Greatness," a young boy is hired for the summer by a silent half-blood to care for her father, an aging mountain man. The story opens: "I was ten years old the summer I worked for old Cal Crawford. For years afterward, I remembered it as a time of terror. I had grown up before I understood it had been a time of greatness, too" (p. 71). This story was originally published by *Cosmopolitan* as 'The Last Stand."

Three of the stories, including the title piece, make strong use of the theme of romantic love between men and women, a theme that recurs in Johnson's work and yet still comes almost as a surprise in these tough, spare stories of survival. "The Journal of Adventure" bears some similarity to "A Man Called Horse" in that it tells of a young adventurer's determination to survive, even though wounded and trapped in a cave as winter approaches. While he is able, Edward Morgan keeps a journal for his sweetheart, hoping it will serve as his statement of love to her if he should perish and the journal be found. He is saved, however, by a young Indian woman whom he later marries out of a sense of debt. Eventually, his wife dies, and he is reunited with his sweetheart. With its theme of survival and its use of a love element, this story is startlingly like Jack Schaefer's novella "The Canyon," but Johnson's spare style is in direct contrast to Schaefer's biblical-sounding description. "The Story of Charley" is an outright love story and it, too, is sentimental, telling of a young couple separated as so many were on the frontier and reunited years later.

Love is a strong element, too, in "The Hanging Tree," a complicated and complex story that is perhaps the height of Johnson's achievement. Johnson, who has said she cannot build a story but has to find one, found the base for this story in two movies she had seen of men stranded in the desert. She began to wonder what would happen if it were a woman stranded, and the pity she felt for this imaginary woman gave rise to "The Hanging Tree" ("Straight Talk," p. 7).

The story opens with the arrival of Doc Joe Frail in Skull Creek. As he passes a cottonwood obviously already used for a hanging, Frail remembers that the wife of a man he killed over a card game had put a curse on him that he will one day hang. Frail, whose real name is Joseph Alberts, is an embittered, cynical, and almost desperate man, playing the role of dangerous gambler, yet knowing himself incapable of firing his pistol. The pseudonym he has chosen for himself is clearly symbolic.

Frail saves the life of Rune (riddle), a young would-be robber also filled with bitterness and a desire to learn to shoot well enough to make a success of killing. In order to pay off his debt, Rune becomes Frail's servant, though the relationship between them is hostile. The action temporarily moves from Frail and Rune to Elizabeth Armistead, who is found wandering the desert after robbers kill her father. Nearly dead and temporarily blinded by the sun, she is brought to Frail and becomes the third part of this unusual triangle. Rune and Frail nurse her back to health, but it soon develops that she has a serious emotional scar from her ordeal. Fear prevents Elizabeth from leaving her cabin. Her condition, known as agoraphobia, was not generally diagnosed at the time, but Johnson was assured by her friend, Dr. Catherine Burnham, a clinical psychologist, that it was recognized in the late nineteenth century. "The Hanging Tree" is dedicated to Dr. Burnham ("The Years," p. 235).

In her isolation, Elizabeth becomes the Lucky Lady of the mining camp, building up a small fortune by staking miners. But the town mistrusts her and is easy prey for a religious fanatic who incites them against her. To save Elizabeth from the mob's anger, Frail shoots the preacher, appropriately named Grubb, and as fate had predicted, faces the hanging tree. The depth of love, which is a factor in several of Johnson's stories, is the saving grace here. Elizabeth finds the strength to leave her cabin and walk to the tree, where she scatters gold nuggets for the miners, who forget about hanging Frail as they scramble for the treasure.

Taken as a whole, the short stories in *Indian Country* and *The Hanging Tree* illustrate several important characteristics of Johnson's work. One is the spare style of her prose. The stories are marked by simplicity in word choice and sentence structure, with the result that action and emotion seem to carry the narrative force. Even the characters speak in short, simple phrases, seldom more than two or three sentences at a time. James suggests that these people are all too busy with survival for flowery language ("Thematic Analysis," p. x).

To complement this economy of treatment, Johnson has an incisive way of giving the whole idea of the story in the first paragraph, then spinning it out. For example, a brief paragraph in "A Man Called Horse" neatly sums up the story of the Easterner who went West in search of his equals: "On a day in June, he learned what it was to have no status at all. He became a captive of a small raiding party of Crow Indians" (p. 181). Johnson effectively uses foreshadowing to heighten rather than diminish the impact of her stories. Perhaps Western novelist Jack Schaefer best described Johnson's style in his preface to the original edition of *Indian Country:* "The stories move, flow forward with swift, at times almost racing, vigor, and then, like a nugget in the rewarding ore, comes the sudden singing sentence that implies more than it says and gives depth and significance to the whole."

These stories are also distinguished by a plot device Johnson refers to as "the switch," which she defines as turning a situation around and looking at it from another angle. Sometimes referring to this as "iffing," Johnson asks herself "What if . . .?" and arrives, for instance, at "What if it were a woman stranded in the desert instead of a man?" Similarly, "The Man Who Shot Liberty Valance" grew out of her "iffing" on what could be done with the old and trite shootout scene ("The Years," p. 332). Neither the switch nor the spare style is as pronounced in Johnson's other works as in the historical Western short stories.

Description is bare to nonexistent in these stories. The opening paragraph of "The Hanging Tree" has more description than usual: "Just before the road dipped down to the gold camp on Skull Creek, it crossed the brow of a barren hill and went under the out-thrust bough of a great cottonwood tree" (p. 132). Johnson freely admits to her failure to describe, saying she doesn't like to waste the reader's time with description. Further, she finds that description gets in the way of getting her characters moving ("Straight Talk," p. 3). If Johnson does not use description, her stories are nonetheless firmly rooted in time and place by the accuracy of her frontier knowledge. After we read them, we know why a welcoming shot was fired: with the old single-shot rifles, it proved goodwill by emptying the rifle; with repeating rifles, it became a meaningless habit. In "A Man Called Horse," we get the details of daily life in an Indian camp—the smells, the food, the customs that, for instance, prohibit a man from talking to his mother-in-law. "The Hanging Tree" gives the same full picture of life in a mining camp, with clear details of the work of mining. Each story is supported by a wealth of detail that creates a credible world and reflects the careful writing of one who cares about Western history.

But it is the people who most distinguish Dorothy Johnson's stories. Her characters are flesh and blood, ordinary people who fear and hurt and laugh and cry. An interviewer once suggested that she writes of "people with no obvious claim to distinction—the same kinds of people who are often satirized for being dull and sometimes vicious clods in Sinclair Lewis and other writers." Johnson was quick to reply that her people do have "no claim to distinction, except that they all have strength" ("Straight Talk," p. 1).

Strength of character is the strongest impression one gets from these stories. Dorothy Johnson believes, with William Faulkner, that man will not only endure but will prevail. These stories, and many of the later works, are positive affirmations of man's ability to meet and conquer the challenges thrown at him. In these stories, the challenges come from frontier life, from a hostile landscape, and from a bitter clash between two cultures.

If Johnson's stories show an optimism about the nature of most men, they also show a strong belief in the importance of bonds between individuals. In several stories, that bond is romantic love, but it may also be the responsibility felt by the young boy in "Prairie Kid" or the duty of the boy in "A Time for Greatness." As Anthony Arthur suggests in an analysis of "The Hanging Tree," these stories go beyond the celebrated Western virtue of self-reliance to show that the fully realized person understands and accepts his bonds to others (Arthur, "The Hanging Tree," p. 5).

Three of the collected short stories—"A Man Called Horse," "The Man Who Shot Liberty Valance," and "The Hanging Tree"—have been made into movies, and several others into television productions. "The Hanging Tree" was her first property bought for films, and she learned much from the experience: "The story was greatly changed in the transfer to another medium. Such changes are supposed to infuriate authors, but in 'The Hanging Tree' they made sense, and I will even admit that they improved it. I wish I had thought of some of them by myself" ("When a Book," p. 11). Having earlier noticed a change in her status as author with the publication of her first hardcover book, Johnson saw a new change in prestige when it became known that "The Hanging Tree" would become a movie. "When a book becomes a movie, even strangers (even teenagers!) begin to act respectful. A book is permanent, but a movie is glamorous, and everybody knows that the author of a story bought for the movies automatically becomes rich. This is not true, but just try convincing anybody except another writer who has found out for himself" ("When a Book," p. 11).

IV — Non-Fiction for Young Readers

Famous Lawmen, published in 1963, marked Johnson's entrance into the young adult field. Each chapter in this book is a short biography, and there is no carryover between stories. The story of Bat Masterson's battle with Sgt. King, for instance, is told in the chapter on Wyatt Earp and retold in that on Masterson himself. Inevitably, because of their shortness, these stories are underdeveloped, leaving the reader wishing for more details and a deeper covering in Johnson's own penetrating style. The premise behind this book is that lawmen had to deal with rough, tough lawbreakers and lived with danger, but the forces that shaped these men are now gone, as is the frontier. Today, these lawmen would be out of place. Johnson included a helpful glossary entitled "Some Useful Explanations," in which she distinguishes between marshals and sheriffs, petit jury and grand jury, and points out, among other things, that rustling refers to the theft of cattle but not of horses.

Some Went West (1967), her second book for young adults, enabled Johnson to use some of the research done for the short stories. In the introduction to this book about women who went west, Johnson propounds her theory about strength: "Cowards never started and weaklings fell by the way." It was, she writes, harder for women who, being more conservative, were less likely to seek adventure (p. vii).

The book is divided into sections, such as "Some Were Captured by Indians," which contains the stories of Cynthia Ann Parker and Fanny Kelly among others, or "Some Married Badmen," which includes Electa Plummer and Maria Virginia Slade, wife of Joe Slade. One of the most dramatic stories is that of Molly Slade's frantic but futile ride to forestall the hanging of her husband, a lawman who had killed at least twenty-six men. Of course, Elizabeth Custer is included, portrayed as loyal whether her husband was right or wrong, and so is Dr. Bethenia Owens-Adair, a physician and sufragette whom Johnson clearly admires. Once, she writes, Dr. Owens-Adair defended a skating rink against charges of immorality: "What kind of improper behavior, for goodness sake," wonders Johnson, "is possible on skates?" (p. 99).

The stories in *Some Went West* are rich in details which culminate in a clear picture of life on the frontier. There are descriptions of chinking a cabin, churning butter, making soap, and baking bread with homemade yeast. A description of Nannie Alderson's remote life on a ranch leads to a discourse on the difference that sewing machines and paper patterns made in the quality of life. Johnson has a ingrained appreciation for the importance of such conveniences. Her tone throughout this book is casual and informal, full of asides as through she were talking to the reader. "Flat irons," she says, "are sometimes called sad irons. You can figure out why" (p. 159).

Her next book, *Flame on the Frontier* (1967), consists of seven stories of pioneer women, four of which—"Flame on the Frontier," "Lost Sister," "Beyond the Frontier," and "Journey to the Fort"—are reprints from the earlier short story collections. "Virginia City Winter" tells again the story of the hanging of Joe Slade and his wife's bizarre treatment of his body, which she pickled in whisky until the roads opened up in spring and she could take it elsewhere for burial. But Johnson tells the story through the eyes of the Flanagans, a poor Irish family eking out an existence in the mining camp. The Flanagan's situation, with the father injured and the mother breaking her neck to support the family, offers a picture of loyalty parallel to that presented by the tragic Molly Slade.

"A Woman of the West" is a more modern and sentimental love story about a cowboy who courts an Eastern girl, his romance complicated by his autocratic grandmother who takes a liking to the girl. But one of the most powerful of these stories is the relatively brief "A Wonderful Woman," in which a man recalls the time when, as children, he and his brothers and sisters were left in a cabin by their father as he went to search for food. A twenty-year-old runaway they'd found on the trail is left in charge of them, and as the group slowly starves, she shows remarkable courage by bringing home a huge mushroom, eating part of it, and then sitting up all night to learn whether it was poisonous. In the morning, when she is still fine, she decides it was all right and feeds the hungry children. Johnson forcefully presents the girl's ordeal through the eyes of the young boy, but she adds a sentimental twist to the ending by revealing that the girl later became the boy's stepmother. This story, first published in *Cosmopolitan* as "Too Soon a Woman," has also been reprinted as "The Day the Sun Came Out."

Johnson next turned to biography for young readers, writing *Warrior for a Lost Nation: A Biography of Sitting Bull*. This biography of the most feared and talked-about Indian is a rich history lesson for young readers, covering in detail the effects of such tragedies as the 1849 cholera epidemic and the later outbreaks of smallpox and measles among the Indians. Johnson gives a clear explanation of Wovoka and the Ghost Dance and straightforward descriptions of the social organization of the Sioux and of the Indian mystical experiences. And always, there is Johnson's clear voice: "No Sioux who accomplished something praiseworthy would think for a minute of saying modestly, 'Oh, it was nothing really' . . . Nonsense!" (p. 16). Johnson also conveys a sense of her anger at the treachery that led to Sitting Bull's bloody and dishonorable death. She points out that he was not honored with a warrior's funeral; and in a connection that gives continuity to history, she traces the Battle of Wounded Knee directly to Sitting Bull's death.

Her tone is far different in her next work of non-fiction, *Western Badmen* (1970), for she has for badmen none of the admiration she expresses for Sitting Bull or the women who went west or the lawmen. Johnson points out that most badmen died by rope or gun, that none got rich, and that like the lawmen, outlaws were able to thrive only because of the conditions of the frontier. Some of these stories overlap with those in the earlier volumes. Although outlaws are frequently turned into romantic figures by some authors, Johnson sticks to realistic, truthful treatment. "These bloody-handed men were just plain bad," she writes (p. ix), and in the afterword, "They were bold and bad . . . . Most of them had the courage of lions, we have to say that much in their favor. But some were sneaking cowards. There wasn't a hero in the lot. . . . They were men of tragedy, and the tragedy was of their own making." These tales, often bloody and never really affirmative, are relieved by Johnson's usual ironic tone. Of the Dalton gang, she comments that they switched too easily from the side of the law. Her sorting out of the gangs — Doolin, Dalton, and Younger — and her explanation of the interrelationships between outlaws are among the most informative parts of this book.

Seven years passed before Johnson had another young adult, non-fiction Western title published, and this one, *Montana* (1977), was part of a series of state histories issued by Coward-McCann. Rather than being a chronological history of the state, this book describes various aspects—oil, gold, forestry, famous characters—and works the history into these chapters. Johnson identifies herself clearly as a Montanan, using the first person pronoun throughout. And once again, she talks to the reader in light, ironic asides. A chapter entitled "From Hither to Yon" begins with the following line: "Transportation—stodgy word, isn't it?" (p. 62). Her discussion of earth formations in the state begins: "Some people like to explore caves. They are called spelunkers. Some people detest being underground. They are called scaredy-cats, and I'm one of them" (p. 87).

Taken as a whole, Johnson's Western books for young readers are characterized by the same straightforward, clean style as are her adult short stories. Being non-fiction, they lack the intricacies of the plot twist or switch, yet the author's presence as a distinctive personality is strongly felt in the asides and ironic comments which seem to echo the tone of Miss Beulah Bunny. But her young adult books are primarily serious, and Johnson makes clear on every page her admiration for the people of the frontier and her strong affection for Western life, past and present. Her careful research, apparent in countless details, suggests that she considered it almost a mission to present realistic and truthful pictures of the frontier to her young readers, to enlarge their knowledge about this all-important part of the past, while countering the popular romantic notions about cowboys and Indians, pioneers and outlaws. "The best reason for writing juveniles," she has said, "is that there is so much kids don't know. . . . To young readers, the world is still full of wonders" (Letter from Dorothy Johnson, March 1980). The American West is surely one of those wonders.

V — Adult Non-Fiction

The only non-fiction adult book that Johnson wrote alone is *The Bloody Bozeman*, a history of the Bozeman trail. This trail saved pioneers hundreds of miles and two crossings of the Continental Divide; but it crossed the best hunting ground of the Sioux, and the Indians fought desperately to hold onto their land. Johnson's research for this book was — as her research always is — painstakingly thorough. Montana State University made available to her extensive primary materials in the form of manuscripts, journals, diaries, references, and recollections. Some of the research that she had done earlier for juvenile works, such as *Western Badmen,* proved useful, and she was able to use much of the knowledge about the gold rush of the 1860s that she had acquired in researching "The Hanging Tree." Johnson's particular skill, demonstrated in this book, is the ability to mine historical documents for detail and then turn that detail into captivating history.

The Bozeman was a short-lived trail, and Johnson's history of it covers only the years between 1864, the year after the trail was mapped, and 1868, when it was in effect closed. Johnson brings history alive in terms of people, both those recorded by history and those who are "unsung." One of her effective devices for doing so is the following of an individual's life throughout the four years covered by the book. Frank Kirkaldie, a prospector who writes homesick letters to his family in the Midwest, appears and reappears in the book, giving a sense of continuity to the otherwise episodic treatment of history. For Kirkaldie, wealth and a reunion with his family are always just around the corner, but they never materialize in the narrative of this book.

Much of the book consists of a series of profiles, and familiar names such as Thomas Meagher become real through Johnson's detailed treatment. She paints a picture of Meagher, Montana's acting governor in 1864, as a flamboyant, egotistical, and unstable person, and she offers no solution to the mystery of his drowning off a riverboat. Other sections of *The Bloody Bozeman* are anecdotal, mixing accounts of an Indian massacre and of the theft of a shimmy from a laundry line, of the camel train to Virginia City in 1865 and of the Hungry Winter of the same year when the price of flour rose to one dollar a pound.

Johnson is meticulous about documentation, footnoting even the pictures and such incidents as Mark Twain's famous breakfast with Joe Slade when the tenderfoot worried about whether Slade had killed anyone yet that day. She is also careful to correct misconceptions that have been generally accepted, and with common sense she points out small errors in the recording of history. For instance, Bozeman and John Jacobs could not possibly have set out in winter to map the trail, as earlier histories had maintained. Their horses would have starved. The two mountain men/explorers went in the spring.

One is tempted to believe that Dorothy Johnson could not write one full page without humor in it, and in this bloodiest of histories, there is much of her humor, mainly due, again, to the force of the author's presence throughout. But she also includes brutal details of Indian torture and military punishment. That many survived this brutality confirms Johnson's conviction, seen earlier in the short stories, about the nature of the men who settled our frontier. The quotation she takes from Thomas Dimsdale's apologia for the Vigilantes is significant: "Middling people do not live in these regions" (p. 172).

With a narrator's skill for rounding out a story, she closes the book with an epilogue that finishes the stories of some of the figures who reappeared throughout the book. She also comments that "most of the descendants of the Indians who fought so hard for the Powder River country now live on reservations and not so well as other Americans" (p. 338).

VI — Two Later Novels

With the 1977 publication of *Buffalo Woman,* Johnson returned to fiction. *Bufalo Woman* follows the life of a Lakota woman from childhood to her death of old age and starvation on the long foot journey north to a Canadian haven. Called Whirlwind as a child, she is later known as Buffalo Woman because her family was well-to-do enough to provide the Buffalo Maiden ceremony for her. Buffalo Woman is an ideal Indian woman, strong with courage and ability, skilled at the tasks performed by women, proud of her culture and community. She is also part of a pattern, albeit a fading one — first an infant, then a young woman, next a woman of the lodge, and finally, a widow who represents the older generation. She is remarkable in her courage and conviction. As an old woman, she saves her infant grandson from a grizzly, though she herself is badly mauled. Later she who had prided herself on having the bravery of a warrior gives up mentally after their camp is attacked and her daughter-in-law and nephew are killed. But Buffalo Woman recovers her strength when she sees that the spirit of the others is broken, and she becomes the inspiration that pulls the camp together. Her final act is also one of courage and strength: she starves herself to death, giving her food and life and strength to her hungry people.

Throughout, Johnson's ability to see through Indian eyes distinguishes this book. She makes the point strongly that the Indian world was a civilization, with an order and pattern to its existence. Whirlwind's first trip to a fur-trading post provides an example of the Indian view of the world. The girl wonders how white men keep their homes clean if they never move them. These are the first permanent buildings she has ever seen, and she soon discovers that they aren't kept clean. To her, they are dirty and smell bad.

This novel, historical fiction in the truest sense, chronicles the real people and battles of the Lakotas. Inevitably, it is the story of the distintegration of a culture. Whirlwind, as a child, is a member of a prosperous family and lives a comfortable life. In her final days, she is part of a ragged band trying to reach Canada before the soldiers catch them. But even as her culture disintegrates around her, Buffalo Woman has a strong belief system. She retains pride in the way she has lived, and she waits for her chance to go to the Land of Many Lodges where she will, she knows, be reunited with her loved ones.

All the Buffalo Returning (1979) picks up where *Buffalo Woman* ended, with the Lakotas settled in Canada where there is further dissolution of their culture. Warfare is not allowed, so the young Indians have no way to prove their honor and are discontented. Eventually, a lack of buffalo coupled with the frustration of the young men forces the Lakotas to return to the United States. The misery of life on reservations, with white people's blind attempts to impress white culture on Indians, is graphically portrayed by Johnson. The sun dance, for instance, was prohibited by government officials because at the ceremony the whites saw only bloody self-torture, not the courage and renewal of spiritual life that made the Indians strong.

The focus of this book is Stormy, Whirlwind Woman's grandson who was only eight when she died. Stormy is sent to an Indian school in Pennsylvania where he surreptitiously clings to the old ways in the midst of a white world. After school, Stormy tries living like a white man, but always with the goal of gaining as much experience as possible to make him useful to his people. He returns to the reservation just as news of Wovoka is spreading. On the reservation, he finds only misery—tough beef and fry bread to eat, sickly children and old people who cannot survive any illness. He feels unneeded, as though his years at the white school were of no avail, and he has lost his faith in the old gods, with the result that now he can believe in neither the white god nor the Indian one. Feeling useless, he works for a white trader who cheats him.

Stormy recovers his faith when he travels, illegally, with his family to Pine Ridge for Wovoka's Ghost Dance. Made dangerous by the possibility of soldiers chasing them, the journey of Stormy and his family fulfills the Indian way of life by calling for the courage which gives meaning to life. *All the Buffalo Returning* ends with that most tragic event, the massacre at Wounded Knee, in which Stormy and all his family are killed. But, dying, Stormy realizes he will be with Buffalo Woman and the others in the Land of Many Lodges. Both this book and *Buffalo Woman* end with physical defeat and death, but that death equals spiritual renewal for the characters, and both books are strongly affirmative. Like the short stories, they tell of strong people who meet with grace whatever life deals them.

These novels, characterized by Johnson's strong, clean prose and a straightforward story line, without the "twist" of the short stories, are strong and sympathetic additions to the body of fiction about the plight of the American Indian in the last century.

VII—Non-Western and Uncollected Works

Although she has said she is most comfortable writing about the American West of the nineteenth century, Johnson is by no means exclusively a Western writer. In fact, the number and diversity of her non-Western writing is staggering. However, only four of her books may be called non-Western, and three of those are young adult works dealing with Greece.

"Going to Greece," she once wrote, "is like returning to my heart's home. . . . I am in love with Greece, ancient and modern" (Letter from Johnson, March 1980). Her fifth and sixth books, both published in 1964, grew out of a 1962 trip to Greece. The first, *Greece: Wonderland of the Past and Present,* is an illustrated description of the country. The second, *Farewell to Troy,* is a novel which uses the Trojan War for a background and tells, in first person, the story of a grandson of Priam who sets out to seek a new Troy. This book effectively untangles the complicated story of the Trojan War and the lives of the heroes of *The Aeneid* and *The Iliad.* The third book about Greece, *Witch Princess* (1967), tells the story of Medea from the viewpoint of Daphne, one of her handmaidens. Like the other two, this book is solidly grounded in a thorough knowledge of ancient Greek mythology and literature.

Johnson herself does not claim any connection between her Western writing and her books on Greece, although she points out that actress Judith Anderson, famous for her interpretation of Greek tragedy, sees such a connection. Anderson played the old hag in the movie version of "A Man Called Horse," and Johnson remembers reading that the actress compared Achilles and the heroes of the Trojan War with the heroes of the old frontier (Letter from Johnson, March 1980). And at least one reviewer has also seen a connection between Johnson's Western work and the Greek classics. Of *Buffalo Woman,* William Kittredge wrote, "It is an enormous tragic story. There is an Iliad in it, and while Dorothy Johnson isn't Homer, she is sure enough ours . . . and her telling is powerful enough for now" (*The Missoulian,* June 9, 1979, A-15). It is not implausible to see a connection between Johnson's strong admiration for the courage of the people of the American frontier and her fascination with Greek heroes.

A book that truly defies classification is *The Bedside Book of Bastards* (1973), which Johnson wrote with a friend, R. T. Turner, Professor of History at the University of Montana. Johnson claims that Turner used to come into the faculty lunchroom muttering, "I'll kill the bastards." He often talked about writing a book about these bastards, and Johnson finally persuaded him to work on it. According to her, the bastards he referred to in his mutterings were fellow faculty members, but the co-authors thought it best to omit any mention of them (Letter from Johnson, March 1980). The dedication and preface clearly set the ironic and humorous tone. Dedicated to a long list of people culled from their address books by Johnson and Turner, the book opens with a sketch of Parysatis, a fourth century B.C. Persian princess, and closes with one of Liver Eating Johnson, the only representative of the American West in the collection. At the end of their book, Johnson and Turner leave a space for the gentle reader to list eligible nominees for infamy.

Most of Johnson's uncollected short stories are of limited interest in a survey of her work as a Western writer because they deal with wartime circumstances and daily life in New York during the 1940s. "Date with a Soldier" (*Saturday Evening Post,* May 15, 1943) is typical. It tells of a girl's reunion with a soldier friend on leave. Their quiet evening is interrupted by a practice air raid alert. The heroine must don her steel helmet and gas mask and hurry out to perform her assigned duties as a warden. Afraid that her soldier may ridicule her, as many civilians did ridicule Civil Defense volunteers, she is pleasantly surprised to find that he admires her wartime effort, and the story ends on a sentimental note: he promises to be home for dinner as soon as the war is over, and she promises to have it ready. An important aspect of this story is that it makes vivid the seriousness with which air raid wardens took their duties, a subject Johnson knew well from her own experience.

An indefatigable writer who freely confesses that she likes to write, Johnson has also written an enormous quantity of articles, book reviews, and letters, most of them so far uncollected and many unrelated to Western subjects. In addition, she published countless pieces under her by-line and under pseudonyms during her years as editor of *The Woman.*

One of her personal favorites, "Miss Appleknocker Gets the Story" (*A Century of Montana Journalism,* pp. 133-37), is typical of the humor she sees in her own adventures. Styling herself as Miss Appleknocker, she tells of her efforts to complete an assigned story about the designer fashion industry on the Greek island of Mykonos, an effort complicated by language barriers to which she took a heretical approach.

Another typical article is "Ruder's Pulitzer Nomination" (*Century,* pp. 138-42), in which she chronicles the difficulty she had nominating Mel Ruder, editor of *The Hungry Horse News,* for a Pulitzer Prize for his coverage of the disastrous 1964 floods in Montana. "There wasn't any book called *Pulitzer Nominating Made Easy.* The School of Journalism doesn't give a course in it. There's not much call for it really. But when you want to know, you want to know" (p. 138).

Among the uncollected works are Johnson's letters. She is, to quote her biographer, "an enthusiastic writer of letters to newspaper editors" ("The Years," p. 381), and she writes on every subject from the needless change of a street name to taxes and water fluoridation. Although they sometimes have a touch of humor, these letters are invariably serious in intent and reflect considerable thought about and study of the problem under discussion.

Johnson also writes lengthy and interesting personal letters, and I hope that one day there will be a collection of these. A passage from her 1979 Christmas letter illustrates the humor in her letters: "A newspaper feature described me as 'sometimes crusty.' This delights me, and I'm developing crustiness as a hobby. My front yard needs a warning sign anyway. It should read: 'DANGER. Septuagenarian—sometimes crusty.' That would be a 10-foot crocodile agitated by a scale infection."

VIII—Conclusion

Unfortunately, not much critical material, beyond book reviews, is readily available to guide the student of Johnson's work; and assessing her contribution to Western American literature is difficult, complicated by the broad range of her accomplishment. There is no easy pigeonhole into which to fit her as a writer, nor is there a school of writers with which to associate her. Denying knowledge of such schools, she said, "When I was writing Western short stories anyone who wrote Westerns was not quite respectable, so maybe I did belong to the Disreputable School" (Letter from Dorothy Johnson, March 1980). But without the qualification that she also writes about other places, she cannot even be called a Western writer. Witness, for example, the New York World War II setting of her latest work-in-progress.

Johnson does belong to the slim but strong tradition of women who have written about the West, and in that capacity she joins such authors as Helen Hunt Jackson, Mary Hallock Foote, Willa Cather, Mari Sandoz, and others. In the 1950s, when Johnson wrote her Western stories, the woman's point of view in the popular Western was rare to nonexistent, as it is today, and Johnson's use of it in frontier stories is a real contribution. She stands apart from many of her sister Western writers, however, in her ability to present with equal skill both the woman's point of view and the man's.

Johnson considers herself a popular writer, shying away from the scholarly. In a letter to me (April 1979), she has professed surprise at the things a scholar sees in her work, and she has denied the use of symbolism, once arguing with a critic who insisted on a symbolic interpretation of the short stories. Rather than symbolic stories threaded with deep meaning, her work, she insists, should be taken at her own evaluation as "crackin' good stories about real people, courageous people" (Letter from Johnson, July 1979). The obvious symbolism of "The Hanging Tree" is probably the major exception.

The thread that ties Johnson's diverse works together is her own personality as it is revealed in her writing. For all her hardcore realism, she has a sentimental streak that wants life to turn out right for people, as it does for most of Beulah Bunny's students and even for Horse and Doc Frail. But Johnson accepts that life does not always turn out to be a sentimentalist's dream, and she is able to present its disappointments, large and small, with an ironic humor that softens their blows. She uses that same humor to cut through pretense and misconception, revealing people and situations with a clear logic. This rich sense of humor is also revealed in her ability to laugh both at herself and the world. Her ironic tone effectively breaks the tension of her tautest stories at precisely the right moment; in lighter pieces, it reveals itself as a sense of outright laughter.

Johnson believes strongly in such old-fashioned virtues as courage, strength, honor, and integrity; and she brings these values to life in characters like Horse or Whirlwind Woman or a tough lawman or a determined pioneer wife. The weaknesses of Doc Frail and Elizabeth Armistead only seem to be exceptions. These characters, too, find strength when it is needed. Perhaps the fact that Dorothy Johnson has no time for weaklings explains in part her fascination with the

West of the last century. She admires the strength of character of the people who survived there.

Her work, particularly the short stories, has a power and impact that often overwhelm the new reader. Yet today, her short stories, for which she is rightly best known, are most familiar in the movie versions of them. It is a mistake to allow her work to remain in such obscurity that she is recognized by many only when one says, "You remember the movie, don't you?"

Selected Bibliography

WORKS BY DOROTHY M. JOHNSON

BOOKS

All the Buffalo Returning. New York: Dodd, Mead & Co., 1979.
The Bedside Book of Bastards, with R. T. Turner. New York: McGraw-Hill Co., 1973.
Beulah Bunny Tells All. New York: Wm. Morrow & Co., 1942.
The Bloody Bozeman. New York: McGraw-Hill Co., 1971.
Buffalo Woman. New York: Dodd, Mead & Co., 1977.
Famous Lawmen of the Old West. New York: Dodd, Mead & Co., 1963.
Farewell to Troy. Boston: Houghton Mifflin Co., 1964.
Flame on the Frontier. New York: Dodd, Mead & Co., 1967.
Greece: Wonderland of the Past and Present. New York: Dodd, Mead & Co., 1964.
The Hanging Tree. New York: Ballantine, 1957.
Indian Country. New York: Ballantine, 1953.
Montana. New York: Coward-McCann, 1977.
Sitting Bull: Warrior for a Lost Nation. New York: Westminster Press, 1969.
Some Went West. New York: Dodd, Mead & Co., 1967.
Western Badmen. Dodd, Mead & Co., 1970.
Witch Princess. Boston: Houghton Mifflin Co., 1967.

UNCOLLECTED STORIES, ARTICLES

Because of the volume of Johnson's individual publications, only selected stories, articles, and reviews are listed here, chosen to illustrate the variety of her interests and publications. A more complete bibliography, through 1968 only, is found in Stephen Smith's *The Years and the Wind and the Rain.*

"A Fruitless Search for the Meaning of Life." *New York Herald Tribune Book Review,* April 24, 1960, p. 11.

"Bonnie George Campbell." *The Saturday Evening Post,* October 18, 1930, p. 14.
"Can We Give Our Children Better Teeth?" *Redbook,* June 1953.
"Cruel Barbara Ellen." *The Saturday Evening Post,* January 24, 1942, pp. 18-19 and 56-60.
"Date with a Soldier." *The Saturday Evening Post,* May 15, 1943, pp. 28-29 and 39-42.
"Difficult Courtship." *The Saturday Evening Post,* February 14, 1948, pp. 29 and 120-24.
"Durable Desperado Kid Curry." *Montana,* 6 (April 1956), pp. 22-31.
"Family Legend." *Seventeen,* January 1947.
"Fellow Has to Get Away Sometime." *The Saturday Evening Post,*October 25, 1941, p. 20
"Ghost Dance: Last Hope of the Sioux." *Montana,* 6 (July 1956), 42-50.
"Going to Whittingham Fair." *The Saturday Evening Post,* December 20, 1941, pp. 20-21 and 76-80.
"Greenwich Village Block Party." *Seventeen,* September 1946, p. 124.
"Hold That Bull." (Pseudonym: L. R. Gustafson) *Argosy,* 1949.
"How to Live with a Mother." *Charm,* July 1956.
Introduction to *The Short Novels of Jack Schaefer.* Boston: Houghton Mifflin Co., 1967.
Introduction to *Vigilante Days and Ways,* by N. P. Langford. Missoula: Montana State University Press, 1957.
"Journey to the Fort." *Collier's,* April 4, 1952, pp. 50-55.
"Killer on Our Highways." *Good Housekeeping,* June 1961, p. 49.
"My Favorite Town—Whitefish, Montana." *Ford Times,* May 1951.
"Number, Please—the Confessions of a Teen-Aged Central." *Montana,* 23 (October 1973), 54-60.
"Outlaw Country." *Ford Times,* July 1957.
"She's Gone with Gypsy Davey." *The Saturday Evening Post,* May 30, 1942, pp. 28 and 78-83.
"The Brothers Left a Bloody Trail." *True Western Adventures,* August 1959.
"The Deer Hunter." *Collier's,* September 27, 1952, p. 32.
"The Elk Tooth Dress." *Seventeen,* 1958.
"The Fearful Hunger of Boon Helm." *Men,* October 1957.
"The Lady and the Killer." *The Saturday Evening Post,* February 21, 1959, pp. 37 and 77-80.
"The Last Stand." *Cosmopolitan,* November 1954, p. 68.
"The Man Who Shot Liberty Valance." *Cosmopolitan,* June 1949, p. 56.
"The Snow Is on the Grass Again." *The Saturday Evening Post,* October 14, 1944, pp. 21 and 41-46.
"The Ten Pound Box of Candy." *McCall's,* April 1966, p. 92.

"This Will Be Mine." *The Saturday Evening Post*, November 22, 1944, p. 18.
"To the Centennial with Papa." *Montana*, 11 (April 1961), 13-21.
"Too Soon a Woman." *Cosmopolitan*, March 1953, p. 86.
"Where Custer Fell." *Ford Times*, June 1968.
"When a Book Becomes a Movie." *Montana Journalism Review*, Spring 1960, p. 12.
"Wovoka—the Indian Christ." *True Western Adventure*, October 1960.
"Writer Recalls Childhood at Rainbow Dam." *Great Falls Tribune Montana Parade*, March 2, 1954, p. 4.

SECONDARY SOURCES

Arthur, Anthony. "The Hanging Tree." Paper presented to the convention of the Western Literature Association, 1979.
_____. "Straight Talk in Missoula." Paper presented to the convention of the Western Literature Association, 1978.
A Century of Montana Journalism. Missoula: Mountain Press Publishing, 1971.
James, Elizabeth Ann. "A Thematic Analysis of Dorothy Johnson's Fiction." Unpublished master's thesis, Colorado State University (Fort Collins), 1971.
Schaefer, Jack. Introduction to *Indian Country*. New York: Ballantine, 1953.
Smith, Stephen. "The Years and the Wind and the Rain: A Biography of Dorothy M. Johnson." Unpublished master's thesis, University of Montana, 1969.
Wright, Kathryn. "Dorothy Johnson's Tips on Fiction Writing." *The Billings Gazette Midland Empire Magazine*, September 2, 1962.

REVIEWS

Agnew, Seth. Review of *Indian Country*. *Saturday Review*, August 8, 1953, p. 16.
Frederick, John T. "Worthy Westerns." *The English Journal*, 43 (September 1954), 282-83.
Capps, Benjamin. Review of *Indian Country*. *Fort Worth Star Telegram*, June 5, 1977.
Anonymous review of *Indian Country*. *The Denver Post*, April 27, 1977.
Kittredge, William. Review of *All The Buffalo Returning*. *The Missoulian*, June 9, 1979, A-15.

CARNEGIE LIBRARY
BIG TIMBER, MT 59011